DATE

David A. Poulsen

coolreading.com

Later Literacy

At **coolreading.com**, we know the importance of reading and writing. We know that you've been told that it's important, too. It's a lot easier to get excited about reading if you like the story! We hope you're enjoying this book — we work hard to make reading fun for you! And if you want to turn your computer into an awesome writing tool, we've got some great software – ***coolwriting*** – to help student writers with stories, poems and essays.

At coolreading.com, we're committed to making reading and writing fun and easy! Visit coolreading.com to try a demo of our great writing software.

come into the cool

If you're enjoying this book and looking for others in the series or others like it, they're available in bookstores everywhere. For a list of stores in your area where you can get these great books, go to:

www.coolreading.com

by
Anthony
Hampshire

Eddie Stewart is a young man in a hurry. He has the talent and desire to become a top professional racing driver. What he doesn't have is the money. To make it to the pro ranks, Eddie will need skill, nerve, and the support of his closest friends.

Books Available: *Fast Track*
Full Throttle
Books 3 & 4 available
Spring 2001!

by
David A.
Poulsen

Lawrence High is your typical high school. Hanging out with friends is important. And like many schools, sports are important. At Lawrence, sports are very important! Come join the Lawrence High gang in these exciting adventures surrounding various sports.

Books Available: *Wild Thing*
Blind Date
Books 3 & 4 available
Spring 2001!

by
Sigmund
Brouwer

The Short Cuts Series sets high energy action adventure mysteries in the intense world of extreme sports. From snowboarding to mountain biking, scuba diving to skydiving, the action is extreme!

Books Available: *Rippin'*
Cliff Dive
Chute Roll
Off The Wall

BLIND DATE

DAVID A. POULSEN

BLIND DATE

Published by coolreading.com, Red Deer, Alberta, Canada

Managing Editor: Mike Kooman.

Canadian Cataloguing in Publication Data

Poulsen, David A., 1946–
Blind date

(Lawrence High yearbook series)
ISBN 1-55305-010-X

1. Blind–Juvenile fiction. I. Title. II. Series: Poulsen, David A., 1946– Lawrence High yearbook series.

PS8581.O848B56 2000   jC813'.54   C00-910606-5
PZ7.P863Bl 2000

Printed in Canada

To Martyn
Who will always be remembered by the
writers he inspired
And the kids who loved him.

I was stretched out under my car staring up at the oil pan. My best friend, Marcel Boileau, was sitting on the fender. He wasn't saying anything, but I knew it was just a matter of time.

Marcel is his name, but that isn't what I call him. That isn't what anybody calls him. As long as he's lived out here, he's been called French. Since he comes from Quebec, I guess it's an OK nickname. French doesn't seem to care about it one way or the other. Of course, I've never actually asked him about it.

We both go to Lawrence High and we play on the same hockey team, the Capitol Hill Eagles. Even though I'm in eleventh grade, and French is only in tenth, we hang out together quite a bit.

He lives about a block from my house so he comes over most Saturdays and watches me work on the car. That's what he was doing that particular Saturday. Or at least that was part of it.

I figured something was up when he showed up with a couple of Slurpees. He never does that. In fact, usually after we have a hockey game, he's trying to get one of us to buy him a Slurpee.

Anyway, there we were on one of those February days that feels more like May. French was perched on the fender, and I was under the Meteor. Both of us were sucking on Slurpees—which isn't easy to do when you're underneath a car.

The Meteor, by the way, is a '58 two-door hardtop with original paint and upholstery and 289 cubes under the hood. I've been restoring it for almost two years now.

"I need a favor," French said after a while.

"Yeah?" I said. "Hey, do you see a five-eighths boxend in my tool box?"

I could hear him clattering around for a while. Then he slid it to me along the pavement.

"Thanks," I said.

"So how about it?" he asked.

"How about what?"

"The favor I asked you about," he said. "Will you do it?"

"How should I know? I don't even know what it is yet."

"It's no big deal."

"Yeah, right." I had to turn my head and spit because a clump of greasy dirt fell off the oil pan and hit me in the mouth.

2

"There's this girl I like," French said. "Annette Difolia."

"So?" I was hoping it wasn't going to be one of those "so can you find out if she likes me" deals.

"I asked her to come to our game tonight," said French. "She said she would if she could bring her friend. I told her that would probably be OK."

"So what's the problem?"

"No problem... exactly. I just thought that after the game if we go over to Shakey's, it would be better if there were two guys and two girls—you know, sort of even numbers."

I figured out real fast what he was talking about.

"No way," I said.

The thing is, I'm not great with girls. It's not that I don't like them. I like them fine. And some of them like me OK too. Trouble is, it never turns out to be the kind of liking that goes on between girlfriend and boyfriend.

Which means I don't have a lot of dates. Actually, I'd had exactly two. And one of them was arranged by my mom. Talk about a disaster. Mom wanted me to take one of her friend's daughters out on her birthday. I'd never met the girl, but I figured, how bad can it be?

The adults were in a big sweat that this girl didn't have a date for a birthday party they were planning for her. Personally, I don't think it's any big deal not to have a date on your birthday. I've had sixteen birthdays, and I've never had a date on any of them.

I doubt if this girl—her name was Lucy something—cared if she had a date any more than I did. But her mother cared a lot. And she got together with my mother and... you know how that stuff goes.

Lucy was OK, I guess. But there was a problem. She could only talk about one thing. Television soap operas. She watched them all. She even taped the ones that were on when she was in school and watched them that night.

I suppose there's nothing wrong with people wanting to watch soaps for hours at a time. But just try having a conversation with one of those people. It's about as much fun as a slapshot on the protective cup.

Anyway, we wound up at Shakey's Pizza and Ginger Beef Garage. The evening had been pretty much a disaster to that point, and it didn't get any better once we got to Shakey's. I tried to talk to her about the two things that interest me—hockey and the Meteor. And you can guess what Lucy wanted to talk about.

The conversation went something like this:

Me: There's hardly any rust and the interior is almost perfect.

Lucy: You know, Curtis (that was one of the things I didn't like right off—her calling me Curtis, instead of Curt), if Brett Jones breaks

4

up with Cindy Smart when he finds out she's having Colin Tate's baby, I'll just die.

Me: Huh?

Lucy: On Days of Our World. Hel-lo! You must watch it.

Me: Uh... of course, the motor's been rebuilt but that's OK. Once I get a new distributor and...

Lucy: I wonder what time Emergency Hospital comes on in Toronto. We're moving there, you know.

Me: Serious? That's great. You'll be able to see Curtis Joseph. He's the best.

Lucy: Who? Oh, you mean Dr. Joseph, the new brain surgeon on Doctors and Nurses.

Me: uh... yeah right. (What I was thinking was, "Speaking of brain surgeons..." which I realize isn't very nice. It wasn't really her fault. She probably thought hockey and old cars were just as dumb as I thought her shows were.)

Anyway, after that night I swore I'd never go on another blind date as long as I lived.

French must have been reading my mind.

"It's not like you'd be on a real date or anything." He was starting to talk faster, the way people do when they're trying to talk you into something.

"Nope," I said. "Why don't you get Denny to go with you? He should be glad to do it."

I figured that wasn't a bad suggestion. Denny Hillman and French are friends and Denny's even worse off than me for dates.

"He's going out with Pam Parlee," French said. "It's taken him since kindergarten to get her to go out with him. He isn't going to want to mess it up now."

Great, I thought. Even Denny Hillman has a girlfriend. I must be the last bachelor on the planet.

"Sorry," I said. "I'm not really interested."

There was silence for a while.

"I'll pay," French said finally.

If I wasn't already lying on my back I probably would have fallen down. You don't often hear French offering to pay his own share, let alone somebody else's.

"This Annette must really be something," I said. Actually, I'd seen her at school a few times. She's in ninth grade, and I'd have to say she's sort of cute. For a niner.

"She's OK."

"So you'll pay for everything—pizza, Cokes. I might want dessert," I said.

"Yeah... everything." He didn't sound too happy. "Even dessert."

"Well, maybe," I said. "Just so everybody understands it isn't a date."

I was cranking on a nut with a crescent wrench. It slipped and I ran my knuckles into the underside of the manifold. It hurt like crazy.

After I got finished swearing (my hand hurt and I knocked the Slurpee over), I slid out from under the car. There were a few details that needed to be cleared up, like who it was I'd be sitting with at Shakey's.

But I never got the chance. The only thing that was still on the fender of the Meteor was French's empty Slurpee cup.

I've wondered about it a lot since then—you know, whether it would have made a difference if I had known. To tell the truth I'm not sure.

TWO

We were playing the Renfrew Wolverines, a team that had given us trouble all season. They're big and rough which means you better keep your head up. I wouldn't call them goons exactly, but close.

Actually, I kind of look forward to playing the Wolverines. It's not that I like dirty hockey. I mean I enjoy the body checking part of the game as long as the hits are clean and there aren't a million fights.

I've only been in one scrap in all the time I've played. That was when some big jerk jumped on French and was wailing on him. I got the guy off French all right, but I figured out pretty fast that I didn't like hockey fights. Even though the guys said I wasted the creep.

My problems started about an hour and a half before the Renfrew game. My mom was driving me to the rink. That was the good part.

She was driving me in her 1979 Plymouth stationwagon. That was the bad part.

I'd been bugging Mom to retire that rusted-out, smoke-belching junker for about three years. It passed the two-hundred-thousand-kilometer mark when I was still in grade school. But she says that since her and Dad split, money's kind of tight. So the junker it is.

On cold days she drives me to school, but I get her to let me off about a block away. That's so I won't have to put up with comments from the other kids. You know the kind of stuff: "Hey Curt, the limousine service booked up today?" Hilarious, right?

The good thing about Mom's car is that it gives me plenty of desire to keep working on the Meteor. But, as Mom says, at least the Plymouth gets us where we're going. Which was true right up until the night of that hockey game.

There we were, stalled on Seventeenth Avenue, me late for the game, and Mom saying stuff like, "I can't understand it. It's never done this before."

We'd have been toast, but this cowboy type driving a Dodge Cummings stopped to see if he could help out. Between the two of us we got the junker running again.

I got to the rink just as the game was starting. By the time I got my equipment on and arrived at the players' box, they'd played ten minutes of the first period and we were already down 1–0.

In all the confusion before the game, I'd totally forgotten about the date thing. (Except it wasn't a date, remember?) And I sure didn't have time to give it any thought once the game started.

Coach Reddick, who's always in a bad mood when we're losing anyway, gave me a real dirty look for being late. He didn't say anything though, just pointed at me to get out on the ice.

I play defense, so when I jumped over the boards I went down and tapped our goalie, Jeff Sandvick (we call him "Sandwich"), on the pads.

"Be ready, Curt, these guys are hitting everything that moves," Sandwich told me.

I nodded and lined up for the face-off. Of course, thanks to the Plymouth, I hadn't had a chance to warm up and I was awful on that first shift. Sandwich had to make a couple of great stops to save my butt.

After that, things went a lot better. I got hit a couple of times, which sort of woke me up. Near the end of the period, I caught one of their guys with his head down and crushed him as he was coming over our blueline.

French picked up the puck and a couple of nice passes later, we tied the score. As we were doing the high fives after the goal, French grinned at me.

"I think she's crazy about you," he said.

I didn't have a clue what he was talking about. But later, as we were sitting in the dressing room between periods, it hit me. I almost choked on the orange I was sucking.

Shakey's after the game! French and Annette. Me and _____?

I went over and sat down next to French. He was still grinning at me.

"OK, talk to me," I said. "Who is it?"

"Who is what?" He tried to pull a straight face and look real innocent, but it wasn't working.

"This girl I'm supposed to be with after the game, that's who."

"Didn't you see her out there?" French asked.

"Yeah, like I had time to be checking people out in the bleachers." I slapped him on the head with my glove.

"Well, you had to hear her at least," French was grinning again. "She was yelling louder than anybody. Even louder than Annette."

When he said that, I realized I had sort of heard some yelling, but I hadn't paid much attention. I usually shut out everything but the game when I'm on the ice.

"Was that her?" I asked.

"Uh-huh," French nodded. "O-oh-h-h, Curt," he crooned, "Go get that puck, you big hunk. You're just so-o-o hot..."

"She didn't sound like that at all," I cut him off. "Come on, who is it?"

Just then Coach Reddick came into the dressing room and we had to cool it. The rule is nobody talks once the coach comes into the room.

He told us a couple of things to watch for and not to retaliate when we got hit.

"We can beat these guys if we stay out of the penalty box," he said.

The whistle blew from the ice surface and we got ready to go back on the ice. I tightened my skates and stood up. We started high-fiving and yelling a bunch of stuff that doesn't make sense if you're not actually in the dressing room.

Then it was back out for the second period and again I forgot all about the mystery girl. It's a good thing too, because when you play a team like Renfrew, if you're not concentrating, you could wind up in an ambulance.

We were playing pretty well. I decked their biggest guy, and sure enough that time I heard it, loud and clear.

"Awright, Curt!" It was a girl's voice all right, and since I knew my mom wasn't a hockey yeller, I figured it had to be my non-date.

I ran over another guy and he slashed me as he was falling and got a couple of minutes. While I was limping back and forth in the hallway trying to walk off the pain, French scored and we led 2–1.

I was OK after a couple of minutes, but late in the period I did something really dumb. The big goon I'd nailed before had me in the corner and was really giving it to me. A couple of hacks with his stick, a couple of elbows.

As he was skating away, I gave him a pretty good shot in the back of the head. Naturally, the referee missed all the stuff the guy had done to me. But he didn't miss the punch I gave back, which wasn't even all that hard.

Off I went, for what the sportscasters like to call a retaliation penalty. I wanted to slam the gate and tell the ref a couple of things. But I figured a misconduct would really put me in the coach's doghouse.

I no sooner got in the penalty box than one of the linesman noticed a hole in the ice that needed fixing. That meant a break in the action.

I made sure I didn't look over at our players' box, because I knew Coach Reddick would be giving me "the look".

So instead I kind of gazed around the stands. That's when I saw her. Sitting right next to Annette Difolia. My after-the-game companion... Judy Baird. She had just started at Lawrence at the start of the term. She was in grade ten, same as French, so she wasn't in any of my classes. I didn't know her at all. I'd never even talked to her. The only thing I knew about Judy Baird was the same thing that everybody knew about her.

Judy Baird was blind.

Three

My first thought was, how does a blind girl watch a hockey game? Then some stupid stuff went through my head, like: this is what I call a blind date. I know it's dumb to think like that. I guess it was because I was totally surprised when I saw who I was going to Shakey's with.

About the only thought I had after that was, what am I going to say to her?

I got jerked back to the game in a hurry. That's because Renfrew scored during my penalty. To make it even worse, the guy who scored was the same guy I had smacked in the back of the head.

I skated over to the bench with my head down. I knew what was coming.

"You take another bad penalty, and you'll watch the rest of this game, you hear me?"

I couldn't blame the coach for being mad. He'd warned us about taking dumb penalties, and I'd just taken one of the dumbest. The period ended and we trooped back to the dressing room. I looked over at French and he nodded at me.

I didn't know if the nod meant, forget it, we'll get 'em in the third period, or if it had something to do with Judy Baird.

I never got a chance to ask him because Coach Reddick stayed in the room for the whole break. He hollered for ten minutes straight. But even though I was the one he was really ticked at, he hollered at everybody, even Sandwich who was playing great.

I was glad when the break was over. For two reasons. I didn't feel like being yelled at anymore. And I wanted to get back on the ice to settle things with Renfrew. I play hard and I want to win every time we play, but this was one game I really wanted to win.

That feeling got even stronger after we got on the ice. We were skating around, just loosening up when one of their guys skated up alongside me.

It was number 19, the guy who'd scored their second goal. His hair was sticking out under his helmet, and it looked like he only washed it every couple of years. And he looked like he was trying to grow a moustache. It was pretty bad, even worse than Wayne Gretzky's.

"Nice penalty, Dork brain." He stuck his stick up under my chin. "Really helped your team."

It was the oldest one in the book. Psyche me out, get me mad so I'd take another bad penalty in the third period.

"Just keep your head up, Puppy," I told him. "Or I'll rearrange the few brain cells you actually have. Oh, by the way, great facial hair."

I skated away and we got ready for the face-off. About five minutes into the period one of their guys flipped a floater at our goal. Somehow Sandwich who'd been awesome all night managed to blow the shot and it was 3-2 for the Wolverines.

I really felt sorry for Sandwich. He was the main reason the game was still close. I guess the rest of the guys felt the same way because we played like demons after that goal. A few minutes later we got it back; 3-3.

Now I could hear two people yelling. Judy Baird and Sandwich. Both of them were giving it the "Awright you guys! Way to go, Eagles!" and a bunch of stuff like that.

I went down and tapped Sandwich on the pads.

"Watch that number 19," he said. "They like to try the long pass to him coming through the middle. If he gets behind you guys, we're baked."

I nodded and headed for the bench. The next few minutes were tough. Both teams were trying not to make a mistake that would cost them the game.

Even so, we made a couple, but Sandwich

was huge in goal and the game stayed tied. With a couple of minutes left in the game, I went into the corner with my buddy, number 19. He did everything but jam his stick down my throat, and I wanted to smash the jerk.

But this time I kept my cool. We got the puck down into their end but couldn't get a decent shot on goal. I could hear Sandwich hollering behind me, "Watch him! Watch him!"

Sure enough, a Renfrew defenseman sent a long pass up the middle for the moustache king himself. The pass was a little behind him, and the puck got caught up in his skates. He looked down to see where it was.

Wrong thing to do! I hit him about as hard as I've ever hit anybody in my life. I heard the air go out of him like a popped balloon.

He went down and the puck lay there. I heard French yell "Curt!" and I fed him the puck. Then I skated like crazy to catch up and we were in on a two on one. I didn't figure French would pass it to me since I'm not exactly Mr. Sniper around the other team's net.

And he didn't. Instead, he used me for a decoy and ripped one at their goal. The goalie made an unreal save but the rebound came right to me and I buried it.

About four of our guys jumped on me and I ended up underneath all of them. Even from the bottom of the pileup, I could hear Judy Baird in the bleachers, "Curt Tomlinson, yes!"

In the dressing room after the game we were a pretty happy bunch. We did the throwing snow from our skate blades at each other and a lot of other celebration craziness. Then I finally got a chance to sit down next to French.

"Nice goal, man," he said for about the fourteenth time.

I hadn't come over to talk about the goal. "Judy Baird?" I said.

"Yeah, what's wrong with that?"

"Nothing," I said. "I just don't know what I'm going to say to her."

"Say anything you want." French shrugged. "She's blind, not deaf."

"Thanks a lot," I told him. "I mean, I just don't know how to act. I've never really been around a blind person."

"I'd say you probably act about the same way you would with any girl," French said. Then he laughed like crazy. "Oh yeah, I forgot, you've never actually dated a girl."

"Shut up," I said.

"Besides, she seemed to get along fine at the game, didn't she?" French said.

I looked at him. "How did she do that? She seemed to know what was going on."

"Yeah, I know. I watched them a few times. Annette was telling her what was happening, sort of like play-by-play, I guess. And every time Annette jumped up and hollered, Judy was right there beside her."

"Really?"

"They even got everybody doing the wave near the end of the game."

"Yeah, right," I said.

"No kidding," said French. "Hey, we better hurry up and get changed. It's pizza time."

"Uh .. yeah... I guess so," I said.

A few minutes later I flung my equipment bag over my shoulder and headed out on the third date of my life. (Except this wasn't really a date, remember?)

Four

S andwich said he'd give us a ride to Shakey's. Sandwich is the oldest guy on our team. He's got his license and a car that actually runs. Sandwich is a very popular guy.

I didn't say much to Judy on the way to Shakey's. Mostly because Sandwich's car has bucket seats which meant one of us had to sit in the front. That was me. Judy was in the back seat with French and Annette.

Sandwich dropped us off and told us he might see us later. He let us leave our equipment in his car. I thought that was pretty decent, since sweaty hockey equipment doesn't have quite the same effect on cars as those hanging air fresheners.

Shakey's Pizza and Ginger Beef Garage is a popular place with most of the kids from my school. Shakey, the guy who owns it, has decorated the place so it looks like the inside of a service station. The booths are shaped like hoists, the pop comes out of gas pumps and all the pizzas are named after hot cars.

We ordered a Mercedes Gullwing and a pitcher of Coke. We no sooner sat down than Annette and French got up again. They went over to talk to Denny Hillman and Pam Parlee who were sitting at another table.

I looked over and saw there was lots of pointing and giggling. But the worst part was I was alone with Judy. I worked my brain real hard to try to think of something to say.

"So... uh... how'd you like the game?" I asked.

"Great!" she said with a smile. "You played super."

"Not really," I said. "I could've played better."

It's weird I guess, but I was really worried about staring at her. I'm not sure why, but it's the same way when I see somebody in a wheelchair. I guess I wouldn't like people to be staring at me.

Except Judy wouldn't know if I was staring or not. Or would she? Maybe she could see a little bit. For one thing, her eyes were aimed right at me. I remember reading somewhere that some blind people train their eyes to follow people's voices. Maybe Judy did that.

Anyway, when I did look at her, I noticed that she was a lot prettier than I thought. Her hair was long and dark and straight, and she had skin the color of that light sand you see on those Hawaii posters.

She was taller than I expected, too. Not as tall as me but definitely taller than French. Of course, just about everybody's taller than French.

It was the smile that made Judy pretty though, no doubt about that. It was sort of soft and sort of suspicious all at the same time. Like her face was making up its mind whether to like you.

"They sure were dirty," she said.

"What?"

"The other guys. They were a bunch of goons."

"Uh... yeah," I said. "I guess they were."

"You're wondering how I know that, right?"

She didn't seem to mind, so I figured it would be OK to be honest with her.

"Uh... yeah, sort of."

"Well, for one thing, I'm not totally blind. I can see shadows. They're kind of blurry and there's no colors, but I can see things moving. Stuff like that."

"Oh," I said. As soon as I said it, I remembered that saying 'oh' is a conversation stopper. Mr. White told us that once in English class.

"And Annette helped, too." Judy kept the conversation going anyway. "She really gets into it. She never stopped yelling."

"I thought that was you doing the hollering," I said.

Her cheeks turned a little pink. "Yeah, I guess I was doing my share, all right."

"You... have you always been...?" I didn't want to say 'blind' in case you weren't supposed to use that word, but I couldn't think of another one.

Judy helped me out. "No," she said, shaking her head. "I got sick when I was in second grade. I lost most of my sight in the first two years. The doctor says it should stay about like it is now."

I couldn't think of anything to say for a while after that. I looked over at the other table. It didn't look like French and Annette would be getting back for a while.

A new waiter, Tony, brought the pizza. I knew his name was Tony because he told us that four times while he took our order. As he was leaving, Judy looked up in his direction and said, "Thanks, Tommy." I cracked up, but I don't know if Tony thought it was all that funny.

Judy didn't make a move toward the pizza, so I took the server thing Tony had left on top of the pizza.

"Want some?" I said.

"Sure."

I put a slice on her plate and took one for myself. Judy didn't seem to have much trouble with pizza. It was hard to tell if she was feeling for it or seeing it a little bit. I've been with plenty of people who can see perfectly but who eat pizza a lot messier than Judy Baird.

"So what else do you like to do?" Judy asked me.

"Well—" I took a while answering. "I have this Meteor I'm fixing up."

"Meteor?"

Here we go again, I thought. Another killer blind date conversation.

I told myself if she said one word about soap operas, I'd run out into the street and throw myself under a bus.

"Yeah," I said. "A Meteor is a car. They don't make them anymore."

"I know it's a car." She said it like, how could I think she didn't know that. "Isn't that the one that was only made in Canada?"

I came close to choking on my Coke.

"Yeah," I said, "that's right. It's like Ford and Mercury, but the Meteor was strictly a Canadian car."

"Yeah," she said, all excited. "My brother restores old cars. He told me he drove down to the States in a Meteor and everybody was wondering what the thing was."

"No kidding, your brother restores old cars?"

"Sure," she said. "He lives in Victoria now, but he still fixes up cars. I talked to him on the phone about a month ago. He told me he's got a '32 Ford, totally original."

"Serious? A Deuce Coupe?"

"Uh-huh. Just like in the song."

Wow, this is great, I thought. None of the guys I know even talk to me about old cars. And here's a girl—a blind girl—who actually knows.

That's when I said something really stupid. "Would you like to see the Meteor sometime?" As soon as I said it I was wishing my hands would reach up and grab my throat and squeeze real hard.

They didn't, of course, and I was about to get another major surprise.

Judy said, "Yeah, that'd be cool."

Just then French and Pam came back to the table. I figured French wouldn't be long once the food arrived. The talk after that was the usual stuff—school and who the putzy teachers are and who are the good ones. Then we all hit on what a total waste of time it is learning about Pythagorean Theory and the Russian Revolution. And, of course, we talked about other kids, mostly Denny Hillman and Pam Parlee, who were giving each other major love looks over at the other table.

It was a nice night so we decided to walk home. Judy's house was closest to Shakey's, so we figured we'd go there first. I sort of took hold of Judy's arm just to help her over the ice on the sidewalk.

"Is this OK?" I asked. I thought maybe she'd rather use the cane I'd seen her with at school and at the rink.

She moved her arm and took hold of my hand. "Now it is," she said.

I figured it was just to make sure she didn't fall. But she gave my hand a couple of little squeezes.

Actually she didn't seem to need a whole lot of help—but we held hands until we got to her house.

I walked her up to the door. We said good-night, and I was turning to go when she stopped me. She was holding onto my arms and she put her face real close to mine. It was pretty obvious she wanted me to kiss her, so I did.

Then I ran down to where Annette and French were waiting.

"Pretty good moves for a guy on a non-date." French grinned at me.

I just shrugged. Annette was pretty quiet as we headed toward her house. She didn't say anything until we were about two houses from where she lives.

"I wouldn't rush her if I were you," she said.

"What?" I said.

"Judy's... having a few problems. New school... fitting in, all that stuff. I'm just saying you shouldn't rush her."

I got kind of p.o.'d when she said that.

"What are you talking about?" I said pretty loud. "I didn't even get her phone number. And besides, this whole event was your idea not mine."

"Yeah, well, I'm just telling you."

I still wasn't sure what Annette was going on about. Judy didn't seem like somebody with "problems," even if she was blind. But the next day at school, I found out Annette was right.

I found out a lot of things that day.

Five

I guess Lawrence is no different from most schools. Even though sports are more important at our school than they are at some, there's just about every kind of kid you can imagine cruising the halls of Lawrence High. There are skaters and jocks, preppies and geeks. And there are druggies.

I've seen the stuff around but I've never really paid much attention. And until that day I'd never actually seen a drug deal go down.

I don't usually go anywhere near the smoking area, which is outside the south doors of the school. There's a big garbage can full of sand but a lot of the smokers don't bother to use it. They just pitch their butts on the ground. It's sort of a gross place to be.

The only reason I was in the smoking area that day was to get my calculator back from Jordie Melvin. He'd borrowed it the day before.

I stepped out onto the steps where the smokers hang out. There were about ten or twelve people out there. One of them was Judy Baird. She was smoking a cigarette, which kind of surprised me, since she hadn't been smoking the night before.

The other thing that seemed kind of weird was the people she was talking to. She was a little ways away from the other smokers with a couple of guys I was pretty sure I'd never seen before. They were wearing a lot of leather and studs, and they looked about five years too old for high school.

I was going to go over and say hi, but I stopped. One of the leather dudes stuck something that looked like a girl's makeup bag into Judy's purse. Then they headed off in the direction of a pretty nice machine—a jazzed up black Chevy van.

I didn't bother going over to say hi. Instead I walked over to where Jordie was standing and leaned against the wall next to him.

"What was that?" I said.

"What?"

"The thing with Judy and those two guys in the pickup," I said.

"Oh, that," Jordie shrugged. "She was making a buy. Judy's a dealer. That goes down two, three times a week."

I didn't know what to say. It didn't seem like any big deal to Jordie, but I was—I guess you'd say shocked. I mean, I knew there were drugs in the school, and I guess in the back of my mind I realized somebody had to get the stuff into the school.

But Judy Baird? No way!

I took my calculator and headed off for my next class.

But I can't honestly remember one single thing Mr. Clarke told us in Math that day.

Six

Terrific. I finally meet a girl I like, and she even likes me, and what happens? She turns out to be the school pusher.

I couldn't believe it. For the next few days it felt like I was in a bad dream. Sort of like it was when Mom and Dad split up. I was like a zombie at school and at hockey practice. I didn't even feel like putting on the new distributor Dad bought me for the Meteor.

It was three or four days later, I'm not sure exactly. I was at home staring at the TV, but not really seeing much when the phone rang. It was Judy.

After we got the "hi's" out of the way she said, "I thought I'd hear from you."

"Oh... uh, yeah," I said. "I... uh... I've been pretty busy." Trust me to come up with a totally stupid excuse.

But I couldn't see myself saying something like, "Geez, sorry. I meant to talk to you at school. By the way how have sales been lately?"

So I didn't say that. Instead I went with the busy routine. I could almost hear her thinking, Yeah, right.

"Well, you want to go out for coffee, maybe?" she asked.

I probably should've said no. But I kept thinking about all the times people said no to me when I asked them out or asked them to dance.

"Yeah, that would be OK," I said.

"Great. You want to meet me at Shakey's? My sister can give me a ride."

"You mean now? Tonight?"

"Well, yeah... if you're not doing anything."

"Uh... OK... sure. I guess I'm not... uh... doing anything." That part was true. I didn't have a hockey practice, and I'd already finished my homework.

So, a half hour later, there we were sitting in a booth at Shakey's. The thing is, she didn't look like a druggie. Or maybe I should say she didn't look like I figured a druggie should look.

"How's school going?" she said.

"Good," I said. "How about you?"

"Yeah, pretty good."

We didn't say anything for a while.

"Had any more hockey games?" she asked me.

"No. We play tomorrow night."

"Really? Maybe I'll come."

"Sure," I said, "if you feel like it."

Judy sipped on her coffee. I stared at mine.

"So why didn't you phone me?" she asked suddenly.

"Well, like I said, I've been sort of busy." One thing about me, once I come up with a dumb excuse, I stick to it.

"Jordie said you were out in the smoking area the other day."

"Oh... yeah."

"I didn't know you smoked," she said.

"I don't. I was getting my calculator."

"So why didn't you say hi to me?"

"You were... sort of tied up," I said softly.

We went back to the silent bit for a couple of minutes.

"So, did it surprise you?" she said.

"What?"

"Don't act dumb. You know what."

I took a drink of coffee to give myself time to think of something to say. "What you do is your business."

"Then why didn't you phone?"

"Well... I just..."

"You don't know anything about it." She said it pretty loud and a few people looked at us. "You don't know squat about it."

I didn't know what to say, so I didn't say anything.

"Curt Tomlinson, the big hockey player, that's what people say about you."

I opened my mouth to say something, but I never got the chance.

"Well, I'm not the hockey player, or the good dresser, or the funny one, or the cute one, or the smart one. I'm just Judy Baird the blind girl. Sometimes I get sick of it."

I thought about the stuff that went through my mind when I found out it was her I was going to be with after the game with Renfrew.

"I finally get them to let me back into regular school and nothing's changed," Judy said. "I'm different from you, from Annette, from everybody in that stupid school."

"I don't see how helping those two dorks sell drugs to students—"

"You better go home, Curt," she cut me off again. "You don't want to be seen with a drug dealer."

"I... I can walk you home," I said.

"Don't bother," she said. "I don't need your help. I can get home just fine."

She opened her purse and took something out. It folded out into the white cane I'd seen her with before.

"Yeah, but—"

"Would you just get lost?" Her voice was getting loud again and I figured I'd better leave her alone.

"OK... well, I'll see ya," I said.

She didn't answer and I headed for the door. I wasn't sure what exactly I'd said that had made her mad. Or maybe it was what I hadn't said. Besides, wasn't it me who should have been mad? The weird thing is—the whole way home I was thinking about how I'd like to see her again.

Seven

I got one of the biggest surprises of my life the next night.

French skated over to me during the warm-up. "See who's here?" he said.

I looked where he was pointing and sure enough, there was Judy right next to Annette.

One thing Coach Reddick really hates is for the players to visit with the fans during the warm-up. Even our parents.

But I didn't care. I skated over to where they were sitting.

"Hi, Judy," I said.

"Hi, Curt."

"Uh... you going to Shakey's after the game?"

"I don't know... are you?" she said.

"Yeah, probably."

"Yeah, well I'll probably go too."

"What I meant was... uh... do you feel like going to Shakey's... with me?" I felt kind of

35

dumb asking a girl out in the middle of a hockey rink. I was pretty sure she was still mad at me and that I'd get turned down at center ice.

"That's what I was hoping you meant," she said. " And the answer is yes."

I was so surprised, I just stood there looking at her for quite a while. Finally I grinned and skated away. I looked over at the coach and he was giving me a look like I'd thrown up on his upholstery.

He made me skate some extra laps, which I figured was better than having to sit out a few shifts.

I played probably my best game since I was in Peewee. I scored two goals and an assist, dished out a few nice checks and stayed out of the penalty box.

And every time I did something good, I heard that yell from the stands. "Awright, Curt!"

I have to admit I was getting to like that sound.

*****

I was still pumped after the game which we'd won 6-2. I must've been talking a lot in the dressing room, because French finally looked over at me and said, "Shut up, will ya?"

I didn't, though. I talked about the game, the Meteor and whenever I figured I could sneak it in without looking too obvious—Judy Baird.

The drug thing was still on my mind, so I don't know what I was thinking. I just knew I really liked her.

We came out of the dressing room and who was standing there but my dad.

"Super game, Son," he said.

"Thanks," I said. "I didn't know you were coming tonight."

"Your mom told me you were playing," he said. "I figured I'd come over and catch it. You were great. You too, French."

French grinned. "Yeah, but I'm always great. Your son was the star tonight."

"Can you guys use a couple of burgers?" Dad said.

"Well... uh... we sort of told some other people..." I must've looked over to where Judy and Annette were standing because Dad turned and looked right at them.

Then he turned back to me with a big smile on his face. "I can understand why you'd rather spend the evening with them instead of your old man."

"We're... uh... going to Shakey's. You wanna come?" I figured I should ask since Dad had driven all the way across town to see the game.

Dad stepped a little closer to me and lowered his voice. "I'll make you a deal. You don't take me on your dates, and I won't take you on mine."

Then he mussed my hair and started walking away. "I'll phone you next week, OK?"

"Sure," I said. "See ya."

"Your dad's cool," French said.

"Yeah, I guess he is." Actually I'd never thought of my dad that way. There were times when I still got mad when I thought about him and Mom. I guess I'd just thought we'd always be a family and now we weren't.

We went over to where the girls were standing. There were a couple of "hi's" and "good game tonight's" and French got a hug from Annette. I didn't get a hug, but I didn't care. I was just happy Judy was there. We started for the door.

"Can I help you carry your bag?" she asked me.

It's sort of a thing on our hockey team. All the guys with girlfriends, they hold one strap and the girlfriends carry the other one.

"It's all right, I can—" I stopped myself. "Uh, yeah... thanks," I set the bag down and she took one strap. We went a little slower than some of the other people, but I didn't care.

Since we hadn't caught a ride with Sandwich this time, we were taking the shortest way to Shakey's. It took us through the parking lot behind the rink. We were almost to the far end of the parking lot when two guys stepped out from behind a pickup truck.

"Hello, Judy," one of them said.

It was the two guys I'd seen Judy with that day in the smoking area. Judy let go of my equipment bag and it sort of fell onto the pavement.

"Hello, Luke," Judy said.

Up close I noticed the two guys were large. Real large.

"What do you want?" Judy asked them. Her voice didn't sound real friendly.

"We need to have a little talk," the other guy said.

"I'm busy right now," Judy told them.

"This won't take long." The guy called Luke took Judy's arm and started to lead her away.

"What do you think you're doing?" I took a step forward.

"Back off, Sonny," the other guy said, "while you still can."

"It's OK, Curt," Judy said.

"I don't think it is," I said. I felt French come up beside me. I knew if something got started, the little guy would be in there doing whatever he could to help.

"Curt, it's OK, honest," Judy said again.

Annette took hold of my arm. "Leave it alone, Curt; she's all right."

I didn't back off, but I didn't go after them either. I just stood where I was and watched.

They went over to one corner of the parking lot, and I could see they were having a conversation. More like an argument, actually.

I couldn't hear much of what they were saying. I picked up a few bits of it. It sounded like the guys were talking about money, a lot of money. Judy said something like, "I already told you." I thought I heard her say that a couple of times.

Then I saw one of them grab her by the shoulders. It looked like he was shaking her.

"OK, that's it," I said and started toward them. French stayed right with me.

"Meeting's over guys," I said when we got to the two creeps and Judy. "We're leaving now and Judy's going with us."

Judy didn't say anything this time and I could see she was scared. She wasn't the only one. These were two very nasty looking dudes. Luke let go of Judy and took a step toward us. It's amazing how many thoughts go through your head at a time like that.

I think I mentioned before that I don't do a lot of fighting. I'd rather try to talk my way out of tense situations. This situation was tenser than most, and I didn't think I'd be able to talk us out of it. Especially when Luke's pal, who was one of the two or three ugliest people I've ever seen, made this flicking motion with his wrist.

"Knife, Curt," I heard French say real softly. "Switchblade."

Nope, talking wasn't going to work this time. That's when I realized I was still holding my hockey stick. Which brings us to spearing. That's the name of a serious penalty in hockey. You get five minutes for it.

Spearing is what happens when you take the shooting end of the stick and jab it into your opponent's body. I've heard of guys getting hurt pretty bad from it. One guy in our league had to have his spleen removed after he was speared.

Now I've never speared anybody in my life. But looking at the two guys who were coming toward us, I figured they could do without their spleens. So I speared the bigger guy, the one named Luke. Just above this big belt buckle he had on that was shaped like a beer can.

He doubled over and started making squealing noises. The other guy turned and looked at me with a not-very-pleasant look on his face. The business part of the switchblade was pointed right at me.

One of the great things about French is that you don't have to do a lot of explaining with him. He knew I was in trouble, and he did what was necessary.

He gave the knife guy a two-hander with his hockey stick across the back of the legs. It would have made some of the goon guys in the NHL proud. Don Cherry would've loved it.

The guy folded up on the pavement next to his partner. He was making noises too. Different noises. Together the two creeps were doing a nice duet.

I grabbed Judy's arm. "I think maybe we should be moving along."

We hustled out of the parking lot, past the I.G.A. and a Laundromat and through a couple of people's yards. I don't know if it was having me hold onto her or what. But Judy really motored. We didn't slow down until we got to Shakey's.

"What happened back there?" Judy asked after we got sat down and everybody caught their breath.

"Not much," French said. "We just demonstrated a few hockey infractions for your friends."

I've heard that when people are real scared, they'll sometimes laugh like crazy when the crisis is over. I must've been pretty scared, because I laughed for about five minutes at what French said. And let's face it, it wasn't that funny.

Sandwich was at Shakey's. When we told him a couple of guys tried to mug us, he offered us a ride home. We accepted real quick. On the way home nobody said anything about who the guys were or why they'd hassled us.

When we got to Judy's house, I told Sandwich I'd walk from there.

"You sure?"

"Yeah," I said. "No problem."

I guess it wasn't that smart since the goons must've known where Judy lived. When we got out of Sandwich's car, I looked around, but didn't see any sign of the black van.

We sat on the steps of Judy's house for quite a while. I was looking up at the stars wondering what it would be like not to be able to see them.

Judy reached over and took hold of my hand.

"That was really dumb, you know," she said.

"Maybe," I said.

"Those guys are snakes." She was rubbing the top of my hand. "And they'll be looking for you."

I shrugged. "So why do you hang around guys like that if they're such slimebags?"

She didn't answer me.

"Do you use that stuff yourself?" I asked her.

She shook her head. "No, not any more."

I didn't think there was much point in me telling her that none of this made a lot of sense. So I stood up.

"I should probably get going," I said. "I'm working on my mom's car in the morning so she can take it to some meeting she's got."

Judy put her arms around my neck and kissed me. Like about 8.5 on the Richter Scale. Her mouth was soft and warm, and I really liked the kiss.

"Will you phone me this time?" she asked me.

"Yeah," I said. "I will. I promise. Bye."

"Bye."

But as I was walking home I was thinking, this is crazy; I'm going out with a girl who sells

43

drugs. And by the time I got home I wasn't sure if I'd call her or not.

When I walked in the front door, Mom told me French had been phoning about every five minutes. I threw my equipment in the closet and called him.

He didn't even bother with the usual telephone stuff like, "Hi, how ya doin'?"

Instead he said, "Listen, Curt, keep your head up, OK?"

"What are you talking about?" I asked him.

"After I left Annette's, somebody followed me home."

"What?"

"Serious," French said. "I noticed this van behind me while I was walking. It was going slow and staying about a half a block back. I didn't notice it right away, so I'm not sure how long they'd been back there. Guess who it was."

I didn't have to guess. I knew exactly who it was. "Yeah, OK, thanks for the warning. I'll see ya."

"See ya," French said.

I hung up the phone. I have to admit I was pretty scared, and this time there wasn't any laughing to go along with it.

Eight

The next couple of days at school weren't the kind that would get me into the student Hall-of-Fame. I went to all my classes, but my heart wasn't in it. Neither was my head, as a couple of teachers pointed out.

I know one thing: you can only stare into space for so long before people start to notice. French said he'd seen roadkills that showed more enthusiasm. He was probably right.

I wasn't really bothered by the fact that two gorillas probably wanted to dissect my body like a Biology class frog. I mean, I was worried; there's no getting around that. I just didn't think about them very much. Or anything else. Except for Judy Baird. I thought about Judy Baird a lot.

There was something that was bothering me. She'd told me that her big reason for getting into the drug peddling business was so that people would forget about her being blind. They'd accept her as a regular person.

I was having trouble buying that. If anybody could stand up to the world and not give a rip what everybody thought of her, I figured Judy was that person.

The drug thing just didn't make sense. I decided to talk to Annette about it. Maybe she could tell me what was going on. We both had some free time first period after lunch, so we met in Death Valley, which is what we call our cafeteria.

"Hi," I said as I sat down across from her.

"Hi." She looked up from her yogurt. Annette is one of the school's healthier eaters.

She's also about as different from Judy as Theoren Fleury is from Mark Messier. She's short with reddish-blond hair and a few freckles. We talked about school for a couple of minutes. I wasn't sure how to get started on what I really wanted to talk about. Finally, I decided to just go for it.

"How long have you and Judy been friends?"

"Pretty well from the start of the year," Annette answered.

"How long has she been... you know...the drug thing?" I asked.

"I don't know for sure," Annette said, shaking her head. "I don't think she was into that at first. I saw her with that Luke guy a couple of times. The next thing I knew she was supplying a few of the school druggies with stuff."

"You think she likes it?" I looked at Annette.

"I think she hates it," Annette said in a way that made you know she meant it.

"I don't get it, then."

"Neither do I, Curt." Annette sighed. "I don't get it at all. There's something she won't tell me."

I thought back to the conversation I'd had with Judy.

"Yeah," I said. "That's the feeling I got, too."

Annette looked at me. "But she's my friend and I'm not going to give up on her."

"Yeah," I said again. "I guess so."

To tell the truth, I was still pretty confused even after talking to Annette. I was wishing everything would be one-hundred-percent clear, but it wasn't. Not by a long way.

"French told me about those guys following him." Annette had a worried look on her face.

"Uh-huh," I said.

"You better be careful, Curt. Those two are bad enemies to have. They won't fool around."

"Don't worry." I worked up a smile for her. "I haven't forgotten about them."

I gathered up my books. "I better get going. I've got English first period after lunch and I'm two chapters behind in To Kill a Mockingbird. See ya."

Annette waved her spoon at me and went back to her yogurt.

* * * *

Where I made my mistake is, I did sort of forget about them—the gorillas, I mean. I mean not totally, but what with our hockey playoffs starting, I got pretty busy. Plus, like I said before, there was all the other stuff on my mind... Judy Baird stuff. So Luke and the Godzilla look-alike just kind of went out of my head.

I did actually phone Judy a few times, and we went out and had some really good times. I showed her the Meteor, and she walked around it and ran her hands over it. She really seemed to like the car.

We didn't talk about the drug thing anymore, but I couldn't quite put out of my mind what she was. I found myself thinking a lot about the whole drug issue, which is something I'd never really done before. I knew there were kids at school doing the stuff, and I hadn't really cared one way or the other. But you have to pay a little more attention when your girlfriend is as involved as mine was.

After I showed Judy the Meteor, I worked even harder at getting it finished. I installed the new distributor, totally tuned her up and even did the brakes and shocks. The car was ready to go a few months ahead of schedule. The only problem was, by the time I bought the license and insurance, I was so broke I couldn't afford to drive it.

I decided I'd spend every last cent I had on a tank of gas and take the car to our last game of the year. Sort of for luck.

Last game of the year. Championship game. The Renfrew Wolverines and us.

I was pretty surprised that we had gotten this far. Renfrew was a better team than us. We'd only beaten them that one time during the regular season.

Yet there we were—last game of the season—Championship Final. It was mostly because of Sandwich that we'd gotten as far as we had. The guy had been unreal the whole last half of the season.

And he'd been even better in the playoffs. In fact, he'd already been signed by the Junior A Canucks for next season. French and I were both hoping for tryouts with the Canucks too, but I wasn't holding my breath.

Anyway I picked French up in the Meteor. In MY '58 METEOR! The car's maiden voyage with me at the wheel. And she ran like a dream.

I circled the arena three times just to make sure nobody missed our arrival. French had the window down and kept yelling stuff at people on the street. Stuff like, "Eat your hearts out, boys and girls..." "Are we cool or what..." and "The studs you are looking at will be signing autographs and letting you actually touch the car later, folks."

When a lot of guys say things like that it makes everybody mad. But with French, people just laughed and waved.

When we got inside the rink, I couldn't believe it. It was still three quarters of an hour before game time and the place was packed.

I stood in the aisle for quite a while and just looked out at the stands. My mom and dad were there (sitting about ten rows apart). There were signs all over the place. I did a rough count and figured there were more signs for us than the other guys. And of course, Judy and Annette were there too. Judy was holding up a sign that said Curt Tomlinson—Meteor on Skates. I had to smile at that.

After that, all our attention was on the game. Nobody said much in the dressing room, not even Coach Reddick. I guess there wasn't a lot that needed to be said.

I figured we were ready, you know, "up for the game" and all that stuff you hear on TV. But I guess I was wrong.

The first period we stunk the place out. We were outshot 17–4 and we looked like a bantam team playing against the Montreal Canadiens.

But Sandwich was unbelievable. I don't think I ever saw a goalie play better. So we were only down 1–0 after the first which, considering how we played, was pretty good.

The really bad thing was my ol' buddy—number 19—got their goal. His moustache hadn't gotten any better, but he sure could play hockey.

It was probably my worst period of the year. I don't know why. I wanted things to go right and I was trying. But nothing worked. They scored their goal when I gave the puck away to you-know-who. You should have heard him yap after he put it in.

The funny thing was, Coach Reddick didn't rag on us that much in the dressing room, which surprised me. All he said was for us to loosen up and quit playing like we were wearing barbed-wire cups.

That made everybody laugh and the atmosphere in the room totally changed. I couldn't wait to get out there for the second period.

I hit a guy early and knocked him flat. After that I started playing the way I can some nights. About five minutes later I hit French with a pass as he was breaking in and he nailed it: 1–1.

The only thing that was missing was the sound of Judy cheering whenever I did something good. I knew she was yelling—she always yelled—but there were so many people and so much noise that her voice was lost in the roar.

Halfway through the period Coach Reddick came over to me on the bench. "That number 19, he's giving you problems, isn't he?"

"Yeah, but I'll get him eventually," I told him.

"He tips off his move to the outside," Coach said. "He'll drop his inside shoulder. When he does that, he's going wide. Remember that."

"Right." I nodded.

Renfrew got one when we were a man short so they were leading 2–1. That one hurt and we sagged for a while. In fact it was almost back to what it had been like in the first period. They were all over us.

With a couple of minutes left, 19 picked up the puck at center and came in one on one. Him against me. He was fast and good with the puck, so I kept my eyes on his chest hoping to get a read on what he might do.

He dropped his right shoulder just a little. I remembered what Coach had told me and cheated a little to the outside. Sure enough, 19 made his move. To the outside. I hit him so hard my teeth clanged together and hurt real bad.

Nineteen went down in a heap and didn't move. I grabbed the puck and fed it ahead. I didn't even look at the moustache king as I went by him.

I guess I should have. He reached out and two-handed me with his stick across the ankle. It felt like I'd been shot. I went down not far from where 19 was getting up. He was woozy but at least he could get up.

I couldn't. My ankle wouldn't hold me. I tried a couple of times, but it gave out and I fell down both times. Eventually there was a whistle and a couple of our guys helped me off to the dressing room. As we were going off, we went by 19. He was pointing and yapping a lot. I wanted to say something—you know, just the right words to cut the guy down to earthworm size. But you can never find those words when you need them.

I mumbled something and the jerk just laughed.

That's about all I remember about that part. Everything went kind of hazy. I must've been pretty out of it because I have this weird memory. I was lying stretched out on the bench in the room wondering how I would be able to work the clutch in the Meteor with a broken ankle. I guess you have strange thoughts when you're in real bad pain.

My ankle wasn't broken. But it was bad enough that I didn't get back into the game. I was able to go stand behind the bench for the last ten minutes. I watched as Renfrew got a couple of late goals past Sandwich and I was there when the final buzzer sounded. We lost 4–2. Nineteen was pretty obnoxious at the end of the game, but there wasn't much I could do about it.

Our dressing room wasn't a fun place to be. All of us just sat there in our equipment with our heads down for a long time. For the first time all year Coach Reddick let our parents and friends come in for a few minutes. Everybody said the stuff you expect to hear after losing a game like that.

Mom was worried about my ankle. Dad said we'd get them next year. I guess he'd forgotten that my hockey career was pretty well over since I'd be too old for the Eagles the following year. And the Junior A Canucks hadn't exactly been beating down the door to sign me.

Judy and Annette came over to where French and I were sitting. As Judy hugged me, I could see she'd been crying.

"Hey," I said, "it's only a game. Somebody has to lose. We're still going out to celebrate in the Meteor." But to tell the truth I didn't feel much like celebrating. Even in the Meteor.

Judy didn't answer me. I looked over at Annette and she pointed at my leg.

At first I didn't get it. I couldn't believe a girl would be that upset about me getting hurt. Even if she did like me.

"My leg's OK," I said and wiped a tear off Judy's cheek.

She nodded but she still didn't talk. It was like she didn't trust her voice.

Just then Dad came over again. "There's somebody outside. Wants to talk to you and French."

I looked at French and we both shrugged and headed for the door. We didn't move very fast because I was still limping pretty bad. There was a guy in a suit standing in the hall. We didn't get a lot of suits coming to our games.

"Good game, French. Tough break, Curt," the guy said. "My name's Doug Eastcott. I'm with the Canucks. I've been watching you most of the season. I realize you probably don't feel like talking right now, but I've got tryout contracts for both of you for next season if you're interested."

I can't honestly say I've ever seen French speechless before. But he stood there with his mouth open and no sounds coming out for maybe thirty seconds.

I figured one of us should say something. "Really?" I said. I wasn't much better than French.

"We're rebuilding this year," Mr. Eastcott said. "We're looking for young guys—guys with potential and some enthusiasm. Guys like you. Maybe you've heard that we've already signed your goalie, Jeff Sandvick. If you're interested, I'll be in touch with details in the next week or so. Now, go have a good time. You deserve it."

"Awright!" French's mouth finally started working again.

We charged back into the dressing room. Well, French charged. I sort of hopped. I hugged Judy so hard, I thought I'd break her. When I told her the news she yelled just like she did during the games. But this time I could hear her loud and clear.

Nine

So you can understand why I forgot about my other little problem.

Shakey's was a happening spot that night. Shakey cranked the jukebox a few extra decibels and everybody was laughing and carrying on like we'd won the Stanley Cup. Which was sort of weird since we'd lost the game.

But, what the heck, we did have a pretty good year. And Sandwich, French and Curt Tomlinson, Meteor on Skates, just might be together again next season. All the guys seemed really happy for us.

Coach Reddick, who was probably the toughest coach I ever had, bought shakes for all the guys on the team. Sandwich talked Shakey into letting him dump a bucket of ice on the coach's head like you see on TV. The bucket wasn't much bigger than a slurpee cup, but it was funny just the same. Even Coach Reddick laughed.

Somebody played "Little Deuce Coupe" on the jukebox and Judy and I sang it like we were out of our minds. I thought we were pretty good, but French said we reminded him of Kermit and Miss Piggy.

It was a good party. Afterward, the four of us piled in the Meteor and did a spin down Main Street to show off the machine.

The ankle was still tender but I didn't have much trouble working the clutch. We dropped Annette off first. Judy and I had to sit there while French and Annette said goodnight. Well, I guess they didn't actually *say* goodnight, but you get what I mean.

After we dropped French off, we headed for Judy's place. The whole way she was talking about the car, saying stuff that really made sense. She said it sounded like the timing was off a little. Then a little later she said she could feel a little pull to the right when I put on the brakes, like maybe the alignment was out a bit. Funny thing is, she was right both times. I remember thinking that having a girlfriend who liked hockey and cars was about the best thing going.

To get back to Judy's house we had to pass through a new neighborhood where there weren't many houses built yet and not many streetlights, either. She was just telling me how much she liked the feel of the upholstery, when another vehicle pulled right in front of us.

I had to swerve like crazy to miss it and I ended up on an empty corner lot. I got out to see if I'd wrecked anything underneath when I went up over the curb.

That's when I saw it. The vehicle that almost hit us was a black Chevy van. Two guys got out of it. I recognized them right away.

They sort of surrounded me, one on either side. They were both carrying baseball bats.

"Too bad you don't have your lumber with you tonight, puppy," the guy called Luke said. He was slapping the bat into his other hand.

I heard Judy get out of the car.

"What do you guys want?" she called out.

"Stay there, Judy," I told her. "Get back in the car."

"Your boyfriend's right, kid," the other guy said. "Stay in the car. We owe this little man something, and we like to pay off what we owe."

I should've been ready for it. But I'm not sure it would've made a difference if I had been.

The first guy hit me across the arm. I mean, he really hit me, just above the elbow. The crack sounded like a log bursting in a campfire. The pain seemed to go to every part of my body like it was being carried on flaming arrows. I remember hearing Judy scream. I think I did too, from the pain.

Then I guess the other one must have hit me. I can't remember exactly how everything went, but I do remember the feeling of another explosion happening in my other arm.

The next thing I can actually remember is Judy kneeling down beside me in the snow and mud of that vacant lot.

"Curt... Curt... how bad is it?" she said, and I could tell she was crying.

"They... I think they... broke... my arms." I could hardly talk and I felt like I was going to die from the pain.

"We have to get help," Judy said.

"There's no one... around here," I told her. "There's... no houses."

"Come on." I felt her arms around me. "I'll get you into the car."

"I... I... can't drive, Judy. We'll have to walk."

"OK," she said, "then we'll walk. Which way do we go?"

I looked around and tried to focus. We were a long way from the nearest signs of life.

"I... don't know," I said. It was getting harder to think. "There... aren't any... houses..."

"Curt," Judy said. "There's something we can do."

"What?"

"I can drive."

I might have laughed if I wasn't hurting so bad. Instead I just looked at her. "How?"

"You tell me where to steer."

"Yeah, right," I said.

"My brother and I used to do that in the pasture at my uncle's farm. He had an old pickup..."

"This isn't a pasture, Judy," I yelled at her, mostly, I guess, because the pain was getting to me. And I was scared. Like what if we didn't get help somehow. I didn't think I could stand it much longer. "This is a city, for God's sake!" I yelled that too.

"I can do it, Curt." She said it so softly and she sounded so sure. "But you have to help me."

I guess what convinced me was that I knew we had to do something. We couldn't just stay there. She helped me up and we stumbled over to the car. Somehow she got me inside, then went around to the other side and got in. She closed the door.

"That pickup of your uncle's... was it a standard?" I asked her.

"Uh-huh," she nodded. "Stick shift."

"In this car, the gear shift is on the steering column," I said. It sounded to me like I was talking in slow motion.

"No sweat," she said.

The car was still running, so we were ready to go.

"OK, push in the clutch... then pull the gearshift toward you and then up. That's reverse."

She did that and found the right gear without too much trouble. I had to think about what to tell her next. It's one thing to drive a car. But doing play-by-play of driving a car is a different deal. Especially when your brain keeps wanting to sign off for the night.

"Now... let out the clutch easy, hit the gas a little and... turn the steering wheel to the right."

That time things didn't go as well. She popped the clutch and stalled the car.

"That's OK," I said but I probably didn't sound like it was OK. "Push... in the clutch and turn the key."

She felt for the ignition key.

"Down a bit," I told her.

She found the key, turned it and the Meteor started.

"OK, a... a little easier on the clutch... this time." I must have been hard to understand because I was doing all my talking through clenched teeth.

We got going backward. It wasn't pretty but we wound up back on the street.

"Good, now clutch and brake both at the same time."

She did it and we came to a stop more or less facing the way we wanted to go. To be honest, I never figured we'd get that far.

Right about then, the pain in my arms was feeling even worse, and I thought I was going to pass out.

"You OK, Curt?" Judy asked me. When I didn't answer, she said it again, quite a bit louder. "Are you OK? Stay with me, Curt, just stay with me. You hear me?"

I shook my head and mumbled something. I was trying to concentrate on the road.

"OK," I said, "you have to... you have to pull the gear shift straight down now. You'll... be in first gear then."

She put it in gear and let out the clutch and we were moving ahead. Then Judy added some gas and suddenly it felt like we were going awful fast. It's funny how fast a car seems to be moving when a blind person is doing the steering.

"Left some," I said, "a little more left... OK now straighten out."

Somehow, I'm still not sure how, Judy got the car going more or less down the middle of the road. We got the car into second gear and stayed there. I figured third might be pushing our luck.

Things got a little iffy when we went by a couple of parked cars with not a whole lot of room to spare. A taxi zipped by going the other way. I wondered what the driver would have thought if he'd known what was going on in the car he'd just passed.

The tricky part was for me not to panic and have Judy oversteer. I had to make sure I said things like, "OK, a little to the right."

Once I kind of lost it and said, "Get over to the right, quick." That put us up over the curb again and we were lucky to miss a tree.

That's when I tried to reach for the steering wheel. That move almost killed me. I didn't do it again. We got back on the road and the next challenge was a stop sign.

Judy did a pretty good job of getting us stopped without stalling the car.

"OK... back into... first gear again," I said. I couldn't believe it. We'd only done that once, and this time she fired that gearshift into gear like an old pro.

The problem wasn't with the gears. Or with Judy's driving. I don't know, maybe I was groggy or something from the pain, or maybe I just wanted to get to the hospital fast.

Anyway I said, "OK, let's go." And we pulled out right in front of a guy in a Lincoln, a big Lincoln.

I'm not sure why we didn't get hit. I yelled and Judy hit the brakes. The other guy must have done the same thing and when we got stopped, the two cars were about one hockey puck apart.

The guy was out of his car and yelling. He was almost as big as the Lincoln. At first I wanted to tell Judy to just keep going but then I figured I better talk to the guy. It was obvious we weren't going to make it much further without having a wreck.

"Judy," I said, "I'm going to ask this guy to help us."

"OK," Judy said. She climbed out of the car and felt her way around the front and over to my side. Then she opened my door and helped me out.

The guy from the Lincoln stood there looking at us. He must've figured out pretty fast that he had met up with a pretty weird couple.

I mean, here was a blind girl driving a really old car and there was something strange about the guy with her too. That's because I was leaning forward with my arms dangling, like a gorilla. I figured our chances of getting him to help us were real bad.

"Sir... uh... we're sorry we almost hit you... we... uh... we've had some trouble. If you could help us get to the hospital..."

I wouldn't have blamed the guy if he'd got back in the Lincoln and got out of there in a hurry. But he didn't. Instead he jumped in the Meteor and got it off the road. Then he helped Judy and me into his car and we took off like the big guy was Scott Goodyear.

What was really strange was the guy never stopped talking. Maybe he was really nervous or excited or something. Anyway he kept asking us questions but he wouldn't wait for the answers. He'd just ask more questions. It was weird.

But he drove like crazy to the hospital and helped us out of the car and everything. Then he just took off. He finally had a chance to have all his questions answered and he disappeared into the night. I'll never figure that guy out. I sure would have liked to thank him, though. I hope I see him again someday.

Judy told me later that I stayed conscious until we got to the door of the Emergency Ward and then I passed out on the steps. She stood at the entrance and hollered until some doctors and nurses came and got me.

I guess one of the nurses started giving Judy grief about all the yelling. But she stopped pretty fast when she realized that the person who had somehow got the injured kid to the hospital was blind.

I bet there were some interesting conversations around the ol' Emergency Ward that night.

Ten

I was in the hospital for four days. The cops came twice. The first time I was pretty whacked on painkillers, and I don't think I made much sense. The second time, I told them I didn't know the guys who jumped me. I was worried about what might happen to Judy if I squealed on those dorks.

I hated every minute of the time I was in there. Well, maybe not every minute. Judy came to see me the day after our "night on the town." My arms were pretty sore, but I tried to smile lots and crack a few jokes. I didn't want her to worry about me.

It didn't work. Her eyes looked dark and puffy. I was hoping she wasn't hitting the drugs or something. But she told me she hadn't had much sleep.

"This whole thing is my fault," she said. She sat on the edge of my bed but for the first time she didn't look in my direction while we talked.

"Hey, just forget about it," I told her. "I'm OK."

"They could've killed you, Curt."

"Well, they didn't," I said. I tried hard to come up with something funny to say, but I couldn't.

She sat there for a long time. I was hoping she'd take hold of my hand or hug me or something. She didn't though. She just sat there, dead quiet.

"I guess... I guess we... shouldn't see each other anymore." She said it so softly I could hardly hear her.

"What?"

"I... you're a nice guy... a real nice guy... and I'm..."

"Oh, come on," I said. "Don't give me that 'you're too good for me' line. They only use that on the soaps. Besides, it's not true. I'm not that nice. Hey, I got 68 minutes in penalties this season."

She still didn't smile and she left pretty soon after that without saying when she'd be back.

The third day I was in hospital, French and some of the guys from the team smuggled me in a Volkswagen—the pizza, not the car—along with a triple-thick chocolate shake. They told me it was "on the house," a gift from Shakey.

It was kind of funny because French had the pizza in his gym bag. Sandwich had the shake hidden in his backpack, and some of it spilled on his Biology book. Which, if you ask me, could only improve a Biology text.

The guys had to feed me since it's kind of hard to eat pizza—even a Volkswagen Beetle which has nothing but cheese on it—without the use of your arms. When we'd finished eating, French told me some of my teammates were going looking for the guys that had got me. I told them to forget it, but I don't know if they listened.

Later that day, a specialist checked me over. He said he didn't figure there'd be any reason why I wouldn't be able to play hockey next season. That was a major relief.

Judy came back once more—the morning I was getting out of the hospital. She was real quiet. I tried everything but couldn't get her to crack a smile. I gave up after a while and we sat there for a long time not saying anything.

"I haven't been fair with you, Curt," she said finally.

"Sure you have," I said.

"No, I mean... I wasn't totally honest before."

"What do you mean?" I said.

"About... about the drugs."

"What about 'em?"

She took a deep breath like it was hard for her to say what she wanted.

"You know how I told you I was dealing because it made me feel like I was somebody?"

"Yeah," I said.

"Well that's not exactly it," she said. "Maybe it was at first... the first couple of times, but then I knew I wanted out of it. They wouldn't let me out. Luke said he'd tell my parents and I knew it would kill them if they knew. So I had to keep selling the stuff for them."

There were tears in her eyes. "I don't even get any money. I wouldn't have wanted it anyway."

"Why didn't you tell me this before?"

"I wanted to. I...I was afraid you'd tell my parents...or your parents and they'd...."

"I wouldn't have done that," I said.

"I know."

"Geez!" I sat up straight.

"I don't blame you for being mad," Judy said.

"No, I mean, I wish my arms were working, so I could give you the biggest hug there's ever been."

"What?"

"I knew it!" I was practically yelling. "I knew there had to be a reason. This is great."

"I was so stupid," Judy said, shaking her head.

"So you were stupid," I said. "We've all done stupid things. At least now you can get out of it."

"Yeah, right," she said, but I could see she wasn't convinced.

"Your parents will understand if you talk to them."

"No they won't, Curt."

"But you can't keep selling the stuff for those creeps. You...we can go to the cops and—"

Judy stood up. "I have to go now."

"Judy, just wait a minute—"

But she kept going. I heard the sound of her cane as she tapped her way down the hall.

Eleven

When I got back to school, the best part was that I couldn't take any notes. That meant other people had to take my notes for me. I figured I might as well make the most of the situation. So I got my notes from Pam Parlee who just happens to be one of the smartest people at Lawrence. Bonus!

But there was a bad part about getting back to school. Judy wasn't there. I was worried. After the talk we'd had the day before and the way she was feeling when she left the hospital, I wasn't sure what she might do.

Or what the two jerks might've done to her.

After school French drove me to Judy's house. In a weak moment I told him I'd let him drive the Meteor. It was legal since he had his Learner's Permit, but it was a little scary. French is one of my best friends and everything. But I have to say that Judy, who can't see, is a better driver than French, who can.

We got to Judy's house but it didn't matter—there was nobody there. Not Judy, not her parents, nobody. That was kind of strange. I was getting more nervous all the time, thinking something might have happened to her.

"What do you think?" I asked French. "Maybe those creeps kidnapped her or something. I wonder if I should talk to the cops."

French nodded. "Might not be a bad idea."

We sat there just thinking for a while. "Maybe we should go by Shakey's first." French looked at me. "Somebody might've seen her."

"Yeah, OK," I said. I didn't really want to talk to the police anyway. Not after what Judy had said to me.

"Too bad you won't be able to eat," French grinned. "I'll just have to eat your share." I think he was trying to cheer me up.

We never quite got around to having that pizza. We were just about to pull into the parking lot at Shakey's when I spotted a black Chevy van parked across the street. Not just any Chevy van, but the Chevy van.

"Hold it!" I yelled at French, and he nearly put me through the windshield when he hit the binders.

"Look!" I couldn't point, so I bobbed my head in the direction of the van.

"Yeah, so?"

"That's it! That's the van!"

French looked again. "Hey, you're right. That's the one that followed me home from Annette's."

There was nobody in it.

"Where do you figure they are?" French asked. "They wouldn't be dealing in Shakey's, would they? Shakey'd kill 'em."

"I doubt if that's where they are." I cranked my head around.

"Over there," I told French. "By that phone booth."

French looked. "Yeah, that's them, all right... Hey, isn't that Judy?"

He was right. She had her back to us, so it was hard to tell, but it was her all right. She was handing something to one of the guys; I couldn't tell for sure what.

That's when things suddenly got real exciting. Shakey's parking lot exploded in sound and lights. The sound was a siren and the lights were the flashing kind. Two cop cars roared out from behind a couple of pizza delivery vans.

"She set 'em up!" I yelled. "Yes!"

"You don't know that," French said. "They could be busting all three of them."

"No way." I was positive. "She nailed 'em."

It looked like a scene from a movie. Except this movie suddenly turned into a comedy. Some people in one of those boxy little family cars stopped right in front of the driveway to Shakey's.

Maybe they panicked or something when they heard the sirens and saw the cop cars. Anyway, they didn't move. The cops were waving their arms around, and I could see their lips moving. I doubt if what they were saying to the people in the car was all that friendly.

Meanwhile Luke and his partner were running for the van. And it was pretty obvious that they were about to get away, because the people in the family sedan had the cops boxed in and nobody was going anywhere. We watched the gorillas jump into the van.

They pulled into the street and were going by in front of us. In a few seconds they'd be gone. That's when I lost it. At least, that's the only way I can explain what happened next.

"Stop those scumbags!" I yelled at French.

For a second he reacted about the same way as the people in the boxy car. "Oh...kay... uh... how exactly?"

"Stop 'em!" I screamed.

When I think about it now, I guess maybe it was my fault. I mean, I told French to stop them; I didn't tell him how.

So French drove the Meteor—the car I love— right in front of the van. It was coming right at us. At the last second they swerved. And with a little luck they might have missed us completely.

Unfortunately, we weren't that lucky.

Twelve

One thing about the older cars is that they were built solid. Sort of like tanks. The Meteor is like that.

The van never had a chance. It bounced off my right front fender and wound up wrapped around a power pole right outside a Shoppers Drug Mart. Sort of fitting, I thought.

As soon as the van came to a stop, a couple of cops rushed over. They grabbed Luke and Mr. Switchblade and hauled them back to one of the cop cars.

French and I got out to look at the Meteor. It wasn't as bad as I figured it would be. The fender was wrinkled pretty bad and I'd need a new headlight and some chrome. The two creeps were calling French and me some very unpleasant names.

French grinned at them. "Sorry, guys," he called out. "I flunked Driver's Ed twice. All those pedals confuse me."

I went over to where Judy was standing.

"Hi," I said.

"Did you just do what I think you did?" she asked.

"Yeah, well, it needed a paint job anyway," I said with a shrug.

"No it didn't." She reached out and touched my arm.

"I didn't see you at school today," I said. "Now I know why."

"Yeah," she said.

"You... uh... feel like a coffee or something?" I asked. "We just have to move my car, and I'll probably have to talk to the cops for—"

"I don't think so, Curt," she said. "I've got some things to do."

"Parents?"

"Yeah," she nodded. "I talked to them this morning just before I went to the police."

"How'd they take it?"

"About like I thought. I guess it'll take some time for us to work things out. At least they didn't kick me out of the house."

"That's good," I said.

"Curt, thanks for what you did."

"I didn't do all that much."

"Yeah, right." Judy's eyes were aimed right at me and it felt like she could really see me. "Just two broken arms, a wrecked car—"

"They can be fixed," I said.

"And most of all our little talk the other day

at the hospital. I don't think I could've done this without you."

"Hey, what are friends for?" I tried to lighten things up a bit. She was embarrassing me with all that "great guy Curt" stuff.

"Yeah, I guess so." She started to reach out like she was going to touch my arm again. But she stopped and pulled her hand back.

"Actually, that's something I was wondering about," I said.

"What?"

I wasn't sure how to say what I wanted to tell her.

"I... it's about that 'friends' thing. I was sort of hoping we could maybe be more than that."

"Curt, you remember in the hospital, when I said we shouldn't see each other anymore?"

"Yeah," I said, "I remember. Bad idea, Judy. Look, I know I haven't been much good at—"

"You've been great," she interrupted me. "You're one of the only guys I've ever known who doesn't treat me like I'm 'the blind girl'."

"Then why—?"

"What I was going to say was, let's forget what I said in the hospital."

I wanted to high-five somebody but that's something else that's kind of tough with two broken arms.

"Sure," was all I said.

"I like you a lot," she said, "but right now I need some time to sort things out with my parents... and with myself. Later on, if you still want to go out—"

"Of course I'll want to," I said. "Besides, who's going to help me carry my hockey bag next season?"

She smiled that smile I'd always liked. "If you have someone else carrying your hockey bag, I'll break both your arms again, OK?"

"OK." I smiled back at her.

Judy stepped up close to me and kissed me lightly on the mouth. A woman in a police uniform came up and took her arm. I watched them go for a long time before I turned and started walking back toward the Meteor.

French was standing on the sidewalk talking to some people. He was doing the heroic citizen bit.

"Let's go," I said.

"What's the hurry?" He looked at me. "I'm talking to my fans... oh, I get it... you and Judy...?"

"It's fine. Let's go."

"But there'll be interviews. Newspapers, TV. We'll be famous."

"You can be famous," I said. "I'm getting out of here."

The cops didn't seem all that interested in talking to me, so I got into the Meteor. French got in the driver's side.

"Hey, lighten up," French said with a grin. "We're still driving the coolest car in town. Even if it has a few battle scars."

He was right. The thing is, I was already missing Judy. I hoped it wouldn't be long before we were together again. But, hey, it wasn't like she was moving to New York or something. And even though I had to wait a while, I had a girlfriend. Curt Tomlinson, the eternal bachelor, had a girlfriend.

I looked at French. "So you want a Slurpee?"

"You buying?" French grinned at me.

Like the saying goes, some things never change.

come into the cool